OFFICER BUCKLE
AND
GLORIA

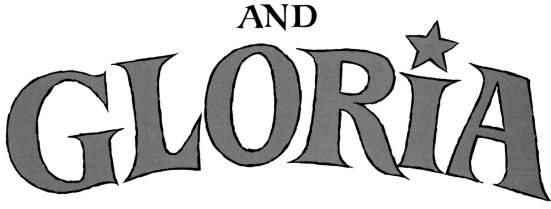

PEGGY RATHMANN

SCHOLASTIC INC.
New York   Toronto   London   Auckland   Sydney

Special thanks to Robin Barnett of Project SAFE,
and to the San Francisco Police Department.

ISBN 0-590-97543-9

12 11 10 9 8 7 6 5 4 3 2 1   6 7 8 9/9 0 1/0

Printed in the U.S.A.   14

First Scholastic printing, September 1996

Officer Buckle knew more safety tips
than anyone else in Napville.
Every time he thought of a new one,
he thumbtacked it to his bulletin board.
Safety Tip #77
NEVER stand on a SWIVEL CHAIR.

Officer Buckle shared his safety tips
with the students at Napville School.
Nobody ever listened.
Sometimes, there was snoring.

Afterward, it was business as usual.

Mrs. Toppel, the principal, took down the welcome banner.

"NEVER stand on a SWIVEL CHAIR," said Officer Buckle, but Mrs. Toppel didn't hear him.

Then one day, Napville's police department
bought a police dog named Gloria.
When it was time for Officer Buckle to give
the safety speech at the school, Gloria went along.

"Children, this is Gloria," announced Officer Buckle. "Gloria obeys my commands. Gloria, SIT!" And Gloria sat.

Officer Buckle gave Safety Tip Number One:
"KEEP your SHOELACES tied!"
The children sat up and stared.

Officer Buckle checked to see if Gloria was sitting at attention. She was.

"Safety Tip Number Two," said Officer Buckle. "ALWAYS wipe up spills BEFORE someone SLIPS AND FALLS!"

The children's eyes popped.

Officer Buckle checked on Gloria again.
"Good dog," he said.
Officer Buckle thought of a safety tip he had
discovered that morning.

"NEVER leave a THUMBTACK where you might SIT on it!"
The audience roared.

Officer Buckle grinned. He said the rest of the tips with *plenty* of expression.

The children clapped their hands and cheered. Some of them laughed until they cried.

Officer Buckle was surprised. He had never noticed how funny safety tips could be.

After *this* safety speech, there wasn't a single accident.

The next day, an enormous envelope arrived
at the police station. It was stuffed with thank-you
letters from the students at Napville School.

Every letter had a drawing of Gloria on it.
Officer Buckle thought the drawings showed
a lot of imagination.

His favorite letter was written on a star-shaped
piece of paper. It said:

You and Gloria make a good team.

Your friend,
Claire

P.S. I always wear
a crash helmet.
(Safety Tip #7)

Officer Buckle was thumbtacking Claire's letter to his bulletin board when the phones started ringing. Grade schools, high schools, and day-care centers were calling about the safety speech.

"Officer Buckle," they said, "our students want to hear your safety tips! And please, bring along that police dog."

Officer Buckle told his safety tips to 313 schools.
Everywhere he and Gloria went, children sat up
and listened.

After every speech, Officer Buckle took Gloria
out for ice cream.
Officer Buckle loved having a buddy.

Then one day, a television news team videotaped Officer Buckle in the state-college auditorium.

When he finished Safety Tip Number Ninety-nine, DO NOT GO SWIMMING DURING ELECTRICAL STORMS!, the students jumped to their feet and applauded.

"Bravo! Bravo!" they cheered.
Officer Buckle bowed again and again.

That night, Officer Buckle watched himself
on the 10 o'clock news.

The next day, the principal of Napville School telephoned the police station.

"Good morning, Officer Buckle! It's time for our safety speech!"

Officer Buckle frowned.

"I'm not giving any more speeches! Nobody looks at me, anyway!"

"Oh," said Mrs. Toppel. "Well! How about Gloria? Could she come?"

Someone else from the police station gave Gloria
a ride to the school.

Gloria sat onstage looking lonely. Then she fell
asleep. So did the audience.

After Gloria left, Napville School had its biggest
accident ever. . . .

It started with a puddle of banana pudding....

SPLAT! SPLATTER!

SPLOOSH! Everyone slid smack into

Mrs. Toppel,

who screamed

and let go of her hammer.

The next morning, a pile of letters arrived
at the police station.

Every letter had a drawing of the accident.

Officer Buckle was shocked.

At the bottom of the pile was a note
written on a paper star.

Officer Buckle smiled.

The note said:

Gloria missed you yesterday!
Your friend,
Claire

P.S. Don't worry,
I was wearing
my helmet!
(Safety Tip #7)

Gloria gave Officer Buckle a big kiss on the nose.
Officer Buckle gave Gloria a nice pat on the back.
Then, Officer Buckle thought of his best safety tip yet . . .

Safety Tip #101

"ALWAYS STICK WITH YOUR BUDDY!"